Hazel
Saves the Day

by SuAnn Kiser
pictures by Betsy Day

DIAL BOOKS FOR YOUNG READERS · NEW YORK

Dial easy-to-read

For Kevin, my good luck
S.K.

For my aunt Barbara
B.D.

Published by
Dial Books for Young Readers
A Division of Penguin Books USA Inc.
375 Hudson Street
New York, New York 10014

Text copyright © 1994 by SuAnn Kiser
Pictures copyright © 1994 by Betsy Day
All rights reserved
Printed in Hong Kong
The Dial Easy-to-Read logo is a registered trademark of
Dial Books for Young Readers,
a division of
Penguin Books USA Inc., ® TM 1,162,718.
First Edition
1 3 5 7 9 10 8 6 4 2

Library of Congress Cataloging in Publication Data
Kiser, SuAnn.
Hazel saves the day
by SuAnn Kiser ; pictures by Betsy Day.
p. cm.—(Dial easy-to-read)
Summary: Having moved to a new town, Hazel Hen makes new friends
by distributing invitations to her Friday the thirteenth party.
ISBN 0-8037-1488-2.—ISBN 0-8037-1489-0 (lib. bdg.)
[1. Chickens—Fiction. 2. Animals—Fiction. 3. Friendship—Fiction.
4. Moving, Household—Fiction. 5. Parties—Fiction.]
I. Day, Betsy, ill. II. Title. III. Series.
PZ7.K6454Haz 1994 [E]—dc20 92-34782 CIP AC

The art for this book was created using watercolor
and pencil. It was then color-separated and reproduced
as red, blue, yellow, and black halftones.

Reading Level 2.0

115-3760

Contents

HAZEL MOVES IN

Hazel Hen was new in town.

She put her best old things

in the best new places

in her fine new home.

"Oh my!" said Hazel

when she put up her calendar.

"Tomorrow is Friday the thirteenth!

I must get ready for a bad-luck day."

Hazel fixed a pot of celery stew.

She baked poppy seed rolls

and an apple pie.

"Now even if I have bad luck,

at least I will have good food,"

she said.

Hazel made invitations
for a Friday the thirteenth party.

"Now even if I have bad luck,
at least I will have good friends,"
she said.

"I will invite everyone I know!"

Then she remembered

she was new in town.

"Oh, feathers and fluff!

I don't know anyone yet.

I will just have to invite everyone

I *don't* know then," she said.

And off she went

to find some new friends.

A DANCE IN THE PARK

Hazel walked to the park.

She saw a rabbit and a weasel

and a swan dancing around a pond.

"That looks like fun," said Hazel.

"It *is* fun," said the rabbit.

"I am Master Harry Hopper,

the famous dance teacher.

These are two of my prize pupils,

Sly Weasel and Mimi Swan."

"Pleased to meet you," said Hazel.

"My name is Hazel Hen."

"Would you like to dance with us,

Hazel?" asked Harry.

"I would love to dance with you,"

said Hazel. "But I cannot dance."

"Don't be silly!" said Harry.

"Anyone can dance. I will show you

how to do the Bunny Hop."

Harry jumped and bounced

and hopped around the pond.

"Now *you* try it, Hazel!" said Harry.

Hazel tried.

She hopped even higher than Harry,

until she got stuck in a tree.

"I will show you how to do

the Twist," said Sly Weasel.

Sly wiggled and squirmed

and twisted around the pond.

"Now *you* try it, Hazel!" said Sly.

Hazel tried.

But she twisted so hard

that she twisted herself into a knot.

"I will show you how to do ballet,"

said Mimi Swan.

Mimi glided and twirled

and leaped around the pond.

"Now *you* try it, Hazel!" said Mimi.

Hazel tried.

She did a grand glide.

She did a terrific twirl.

She did a long leap. Too long!

KER-SPLASH!!!

Harry and Sly and Mimi

pulled Hazel out of the pond.

"Oh, bugs and bother!" said Hazel.

"I cannot do ballet. I cannot Twist.

I cannot Bunny Hop. I give up!"

"Don't give up now, Hazel,"

said Harry. "Anyone can dance."

"Anyone but me!" said Hazel.

Hazel ruffled her feathers.

"If there is one thing I hate,

it is being all wet," she said.

19

She flapped her wings.

She stomped her feet.

She jiggled and shook

until she was dry.

"Hazel!" cried Harry.

"You were dancing!

I have never seen anyone dance

the Funky Chicken so well!

You are a prize pupil!"

"It was nothing," said Hazel.

"Anyone can dance!"

RIP RAT

Hazel strolled downtown.

She walked into a clothing store

just as a big rat

carrying a stack of clothes

came running out.

They bumped into each other.

"YOIKS!" squeaked the rat.

He hopped high into the air.

He dropped the stack of clothes,

and ran away.

"That was a very good Bunny Hop!"

Hazel called after him.

"That rat should join

Master Harry Hopper's dance class,"

Hazel told the salescat.

"He would be a prize pupil."

"Rip Rat is nothing but
a prize thief," said the cat.
"Thank you for scaring him away."
"Hazel Hen at your service,"
said Hazel.
"I am Ginger," said the cat.

"Please choose anything
in my store as a reward."
"How kind of you!" said Hazel.
"I do need some rain clothes,
just in case it rains tomorrow."

Ginger gave Hazel

a large yellow umbrella,

a shiny blue raincoat,

and a pair of red rain boots.

"These will keep you cozy and dry,"

said Ginger.

"Thank you, thank you, thank you,"

said Hazel.

On her way home Hazel saw a rooster.

"He looks friendly," she said.

"Yoo-hoo, Mister Rooster!"

The rooster took one look at Hazel

and ran the other way.

A little black sack

fell from under his wing.

Hazel picked up the sack.

She ran after the rooster.

"Wait!" she yelled.

But he did not wait. He ran faster.

The rooster ran into the park,

past Harry, Sly, and Mimi.

"Look out!" called Hazel.

She was too late. *KER-SPLASH!!!*

"Help!" the rooster cried.

"I will save you," said Hazel.

Hazel quickly put on

her new rain clothes.

She waded into the pond,

and dragged the rooster to shore.

"Y-a-a-a-y, Hazel!"

shouted Harry and Sly and Mimi.

"Why were you chasing me,

you silly hen?" asked the rooster.

"I just wanted to return

this little black sack you dropped,"

said Hazel.

The rooster snatched the sack.

He did not even say thank you.

Just then a policedog arrived.

"What is going on here?" said the dog.

The rooster smiled slyly.

"My good friend Hazel saved my life,
Officer Pete," he said.

He wrapped his wings around Hazel
and gave her a big hug.

"It was nothing," said Hazel.

She gave the rooster

a peck on the cheek.

"YUCK!" said the rooster.

He jumped back and dropped his sack.

The sack ripped open,

and out came dozens of bright blue

and red and purple jewels.

"*YOIKS!*" squeaked the rooster.

He hopped high into the air.

He hopped right out of his feathers.

"RIP RAT!" said Hazel.

"DRAT!" said Rip Rat.

"A clever disguise!"

said Officer Pete.

"But not too clever for Hazel!"

said Harry Hopper.

"She nabbed that nasty rat!" said Sly.

"And saved the day!" said Mimi.

"Y-a-a-a-y, Hazel, our hero!"

shouted everyone.

They picked Hazel up

and danced around the pond

with her on their shoulders.

"I have never been a hero before,"
said Hazel. "I think I like it."

HAZEL'S PARTY

That night at seven o'clock,

the doorbell rang.

"Who could that be?" said Hazel.

It was Harry and Sly and Mimi

and Ginger and Officer Pete.

"We are here for the party!"

said Ginger.

"You are a day early," said Hazel.

"My Friday the thirteenth party

is tomorrow.

Today is only Thursday the twelfth."

41

She showed them her calendar.

Hazel's new friends laughed.

"What is so funny?" asked Hazel.

"*You* are!" said Harry.

"Today is not Thursday the twelfth,"
said Sly.

"Today is Friday the thirteenth,"
said Mimi.

"Oh, feathers and fluff!
I was so busy moving
that I forgot to mark my calendar,"
said Hazel. "Luckily I am ready
for tomorrow's party today."
"Y-a-a-a-y!" said Hazel's guests.
They all ate celery stew
and poppy seed rolls
and apple pie.

Hazel showed them

how to dance the Funky Chicken.

Then they played

Pin the Tail on the Rat

until the clock struck midnight.

"Friday the thirteenth is over,"

said Hazel.

"And what a very good-luck day

it has been!"

As Hazel's guests were leaving,

it started to rain.

"Oh no!" said Ginger.

"We will all be soaked!"

"Don't worry," said Hazel.

She gave her large yellow umbrella
to Harry, Sly, and Mimi.

She gave her shiny blue raincoat
to Ginger.

She gave her red rain boots
to Officer Pete.

"You saved the day again, Hazel!"
said Officer Pete. "What a hen!"

"It was nothing," said Hazel.

After everyone was gone,

Hazel marked her calendar. Twice.

Then she hopped into bed

in her fine new home,

and soon began to dream

about her fine new friends.